The FIDORI TRILOGY

BOOK 1: AN UNLIKELY FRIENDSHIP

BY JASMINE FOGWELL

destinēemedia

An Unlikely Friendship
Book 1 of The Fidori Trilogy
Jasmine Fogwell
© Copyright 2016 By Jasmine Fogwell

Published by Destinée Media: www.destineemedia.com
Written by Jasmine Fogwell: www.jasminefogwell.com
Illustrations and cover illustration by Amanda Kramer Kaczynski
Interior design by Julie Lundy: www.juliekaren.com
Cover design by Devon Brown: www.oxburger.wix.com/oxburger

ISBN: 978-1-938367-25-0

Dedication

This book is dedicated to Blake Allen.
Together, we created the creatures called
Fidoris and I could not have written this
book without him.

~

Pronunciation Key

Some of the names in this book have been inspired
by my time in a small village in the Swiss Alps.
Pronounce them as you wish, but this is how they
sound when I tell the story!

Rionzi: RYE-on-zee
DuCret: DEW-cray
Nemesté: NEM-es-tay
Fidoris: fi-door-ees

BE SURE TO READ ALL OF

The FIDORI TRILOGY

BOOK 1:
AN UNLIKELY FRIENDSHIP

BOOK 2:
THE PURPLE FLOWER

BOOK 3:
THE JOURNEY TO THE
TOP OF THE TREES

BOOK 1:
AN UNLIKELY
FRIENDSHIP

~

The Ghosts of Nemesté

The sign reading *Nemesté* reflected their headlights as they drove by. Bella looked out the window at the familiar old village blurred by the torrential downpour. As they crept up the narrow road, it felt as though they had never left. The houses looked the same, that one streetlight still flickered, and the old inn at the top of the hill still cast a shadow over the streets. It wasn't exactly the peaceful homecoming she had hoped for. They had been gone a year and hadn't really enjoyed living in the city. Bella hadn't expected it, but the old mystery of the village suddenly resurfaced in her thoughts.

"Do you think the old lady still lives in the inn?" she whispered to her husband, David, as they pulled into the parking lot.

"I think so," he responded, though he seemed less concerned than she. "I'll go in and talk to the innkeeper." As he opened the door, rain flooded in, and he was drenched before he even stood up.

Bella looked at James, their ten-year-old son, who was sleeping soundly in the back seat. She worried about him. He had a fantastic imagination, but sometimes she wondered whether he could tell the difference between the real world and the one he imagined.

She turned and looked up at the inn. A faint light glowed from the window on the third floor. *Rionzi DuCrét,* she thought. *How can she still be living?* It must have been nearly forty years ago that Bella, as a young child, had sat on the grass in the park and listened to the old woman's stories. Mrs. DuCrét had been over one hundred years old then.

Bella's mom once told her that the old lady hadn't always been so strange and mysterious. Rionzi DuCrét had played an active part in the small mountain village of Nemesté. She was often seen walking through the village on her way to tea with someone. She knew all the village people by name, and they all knew her, as well. She lived in a beautiful log home that her husband had built for her, and she babysat all the children in the town and made ice cream for them. The children adored Mrs. DuCrét, and she adored them.

The children were adults now, with their own children. Many had left Nemesté to explore the world, though a handful had returned to live a quiet village life again. Rionzi DuCrét had since moved from her log home into the small apartment on the third floor of the rundown inn. She didn't leave her apartment often, and only about once every two weeks was she allowed to go for a walk. She would wander slowly through the town and off into the forest. The village people would whisper about whether she would return this time—and, if she did return, they wondered what sort of crazy stories she might tell.

It had all begun about fifty years earlier. Rionzi DuCrét had ventured out for an afternoon walk in the forest. It was a sunny day, but a chill breeze blew through town. Her husband had passed away a few weeks earlier, and she was deeply mourning his loss. Most people thought she had gone to seek some peace within the forest.

Instead, she disappeared for a year. Some worried she had died, while others thought she must have wanted to quietly leave the village and the memories of her husband. A few kind people searched the forest for her but found no trace.

Then, one day, to everyone's surprise, she walked back into the village and acted as if no time had passed. But something was different about her. She told the story of what she had seen in the forest on her long walk. That day was never forgotten in Nemesté. She claimed to have seen creatures among the trees, creatures so strange they hadn't even been told of in fairy tales.

Even though the people of the village thought her story of the creatures was ridiculous, Rionzi DuCrét was a respected member of the community, so they set out to explore the area where she claimed to have seen them. They searched the forest through the evening and late into the night. The sun had set, and the moon lit the sky. Slowly, the search party began to wander back to the village, though a few remained, searching into the wee hours of the morning. As suspected, there was no evidence of any such creatures. There were no footprints, and the dogs couldn't pick up a scent.

The village people asked Rionzi never to speak of the creatures again. She was nearly one hundred years old at that time, and they feared she had perhaps gone insane.

One day, about a decade after she was banned from telling her stories, she was discovered in the park, telling the village children about the creatures. In the shadow of the nearby church, young Bella and the other children listened with enthusiasm until one boy's father sternly told Rionzi to stop. For a month after the incident, the children of the village talked about the creatures. They played games pretending to be the creatures—but not the same way they played games about fairies or goblins. The children believed the creatures were real. They would set out into the forest in search of them, but still the creatures were never found. The parents and teachers were frightened, and their fright turned to anger at the children's obsession.

One dark night, as clouds engulfed the village, the adults had a secret meeting to discuss what should be done about Rionzi DuCrét. Later, Bella's mother told her what had happened. The meeting was chaos at first, as there was a spirit of panic in the small, crowded room. All the adults were shouting about what they thought had to be done with the crazy old lady. Rionzi was polluting the children's minds, and the naive children believed her stories to be true. Some wanted to ban Rionzi from the village, while others thought it would be best to lock her up in prison for life. There were even a few who thought the old woman should be killed. No one outside the village would ever know, and their children would be safe.

Somehow, amidst the chaos of confusion and panic, an insignificant scruffy old man was heard. The voices of panic began to quiet as he spoke. To the surprise of the village people, this man, the old innkeeper, said he would take care of Rionzi until she died. He, too, had heard her tell the story of the mysterious creatures, and though he would never admit it to anyone, he wondered, secretly, if it could be true. So, that night, he told the townspeople that he would house, feed, and guard Rionzi DuCrét for the rest of her life. They made an agreement that every two weeks, at a specific time, she would be allowed out for a walk into the woods. The time would be known to everyone so there would be no opportunity for her to tell tall tales to the children.

Rionzi had no choice but to agree to the terms. The thought of leaving Nemesté crossed her mind only once, but she had nowhere else to go. She also lived with a small hope of seeing the mysterious creatures again.

As the years went by, the old innkeeper passed away, and his son, Saleem, continued to fulfill his father's promise to take care of the old lady. For many, many years, Rionzi was almost forgotten— but when she turned one hundred and ten, then one hundred and thirty, then one hundred and fifty years old, the townspeople began to talk about her again. She seemed to be living an unnaturally healthy long life. No one would say it out loud, but many of the children from the park by the church so many years before, including Bella, secretly wondered whether, perhaps, the story had been true.

Now, Bella had returned to Nemesté only to discover that the old lady continued to live on the third floor of the inn. Rionzi DuCrét was now one hundred and fifty years old, and it had been about forty years since any of the people from the village, besides Saleem, had talked to her. When she went on her walks once every two weeks, the village people remained indoors, only peering out their windows to catch a small glimpse of her as she walked by. When they had to pass the inn, they stared down at the road or simply looked away.

David jumped back into the car and slammed the door in an effort to stay dry, startling Bella out of her thoughts. She smiled at the sight of him dripping wet. He glanced into the back seat at James, who stirred a little.

David spoke softly. "The good news is that the weather should clear up tomorrow. The bad news is that Rionzi DuCrét is still alive."

"Who's Rionzi DuCrét?" a tired voice squeaked from the backseat.

"She lives here in the inn," Bella said, "but the innkeeper says you mustn't disturb her. She is very old—and very strange," she added under her breath.

"Oh," James said. He wondered for a brief moment who the old lady was, but as he looked around and recognized his old town, he was distracted. His smile stretched across his whole face when he asked, "Are we here?"

The Woman Upstairs

Standing outside the old inn the next morning, Saleem took a deep breath as the Roedeses left. That family had caused him nothing but trouble. They had taken it upon themselves to police Rionzi DuCrét—or, rather, they seemed to have inherited that sense of responsibility from Don Roedes's father. Sometimes they would go months without saying a word, and then, out of nowhere, they would show up and demand that Saleem prove the old lady was still inside.

"Was that Don and Jane Roedes?" David said as he and Bella came outside, startling Saleem.

"Good morning, how did you sleep?" Saleem replied. "Yes, that was them. They pay a visit every once in a while."

"The room was nice and quiet," Bella said. "We slept well, thank you."

"I haven't seen the Roedeses in ages," David said. "Do they still come around checking up on Rionzi DuCrét?"

"Yes, sometimes. Usually after a night where the fog is eerie and thick. They're very superstitious." Saleem worried he might be saying too much, but it just kept slipping out.

"Well, I think they have a right to be worried," David said. "Jane nearly died out in the forest when we were kids, looking for those creatures."

"I suppose it gives her a reason to be afraid, but nobody locked her away for claiming to see a ghost," Saleem said. He regretted those words the minute they came out.

"Come on, Saleem. She was just a kid," David said. "She spent the night alone in the forest and was scared."

David was trying to stick up for the Roedeses, but in truth he thought they had taken the situation a little too far.

Bella stepped in to change the subject. "Well, that's one thing we don't have to worry about with James. He's amazing. He never gets lost in the forest."

In truth, though, she was a little nervous each time he went off into the woods—but it was hard to stop him, because he loved it so much.

"How is James?" Saleem asked. "He has grown a lot since the last time I saw him."

"I hope he'll be okay," Bella replied. "He didn't like the city much. James is a very imaginative boy, and I think the other kids picked on him a bit because of his wild stories. He's very excited to be back. I think he's inside, reading somewhere."

"Would you like to see the gardens?" Saleem asked.

David and Bella both nodded and walked around the side of the large chalet.

Meanwhile, inside the inn, James had stopped reading and was beginning to explore the old building. He climbed the creaky stairs to the second floor and cautiously peeked around the corner. Only a small flickering lamp lit the musty hall, and James thought it might die any minute. He took a quick look behind him, down the long stairs, to make sure he was alone and then stepped out into the corridor. The old paintings on the wooden walls looked older than the building itself. Their white frames had long been tinted with a yellow film from years of dust. James inspected each painting carefully. Most were paintings of faraway lands that guests had left as gifts of thanks to Saleem's father, the old innkeeper. Though James tried to be as quiet as possible, each step brought with it a loud creak.

It was sunny and warm outside, which was a nice change from the freezing rain of the previous night. But this hallway was stuffy and dark, with only one small window. A few of the rooms were vacant, likely to be filled with weary travelers by the evening. James peeked through their open doors. The rooms all looked fairly similar. There was a bed or two, a chair and a nightstand of some sort, and a few old paintings on the walls. The rooms were simple yet clean and comfortable, and each led out to a balcony overlooking the valley. The view was spectacular: a mountain range lined the horizon, with snowy peaks above and lush green forests below.

James stepped out onto one of the balconies and tiptoed to the edge. His parents were still with the innkeeper, admiring the gardens. He was just about to step back into the vacant room when he was startled by the sound of a cough. He stopped a moment and held his breath. Nobody was on the balcony.

He heard a creaking sound and realized it was coming from the floor above him. It was a steady pattern, a rhythm, not the sound of a person walking or a foot tapping. It was calming, in a way. James crouched on the balcony, frozen in fear yet a little excited about the mystery. As quietly as he could, he crept back inside the room and into the long dark corridor. He was thankful not to have been caught, and a little fear wasn't enough to stop his exploration.

Who was up there? Could it be the old lady his parents had talked about?

He continued on, trying each door, but most of the closed ones were locked. Finally, he reached the end of the hall, which seemed darker than before. Right at the end was a door that looked different from all the rest. There was no pattern on it, just a plain piece of wood with a rickety old handle. A metal door knocker hung on by one rusty nail. The old door looked out of place, like an afterthought. Whoever had hung it up had only barely completed the job. At first, James thought of using the metal door knocker, provided it didn't fall off, but he decided against it. It would make his presence known to whoever, or whatever, was behind that door. He approached it quietly and cautiously.

He carefully placed his hand on the rickety handle and gave a gentle pull. To his surprise, the door was unlocked. It creaked a little as he pushed it open and peered through the small crack. The room was dark and reeked of sweat and burnt coffee. There was another set of stairs leading to an open space above. He opened the door just enough to squeeze through, then quietly shut it behind him and tiptoed ever so slowly up the long wooden stairs. They creaked with each step no matter how lightly he tried to step.

The stairway ascended to the centre of a large open room, and he stopped on the top step to investigate. In the small kitchen, dirty dishes overflowed from the counter onto the stove. To the other side was a single chair in front of a stone fireplace. He could imagine that on a cold night, the warm glow of the fire would bring some comfort to the old apartment.

James quickly scanned the scene before poking the rest of his head up above the floor level.

He noticed a door that led out to a balcony, and a large window beside it overlooked the valley. He slunk back down the stairs a little when he noticed a person sitting there. She was an older woman with scraggly grey hair, and she wore a ratty knitted shawl over her bony shoulders. She took a sip of her coffee and set the mug down on the window ledge.

James took a step forwards, wanting a better look at the mysterious figure. She seemed like a ghost, the way she floated back and forth, back and forth. Before he knew it, he had crept up the rest of the stairs and was making his way across the wooden floor, creaking with each step. The door was open, swaying slowly in the gentle breeze. He stood about a foot away from the window when the old woman spoke.

"Are you just going to sneak around my apartment and stare at me all day, or will you have some manners and come say hello?"

James froze. He was caught. Nobody was supposed to know he was up here—seeing as he wasn't supposed to be here at all. The innkeeper had given very specific instructions for nobody to disturb the old lady on the upper floor. James hadn't meant to disturb her. He'd only wanted a peek. Her tone of voice hadn't exactly been friendly, but she didn't seem angry, either. Why wasn't he allowed to disturb her? She had heard him now, and it was too late. He could turn and run, but his curiosity was too great. Yet, at the same time, his fear kept him frozen. He just stood there and stared.

"I thought they told you not to disturb me," she said.

This startled James a little. Although the old, withered figure spoke to him, she didn't look at him or acknowledge his presence in any other way. She continued staring at the mountains across the valley and rocking in her rocking chair. James wondered whether she actually knew he was there or was just talking to herself. He stood just inside the door for a moment longer.

"They call you James, is that right?"

"Yes," he said. He quickly covered his mouth when he realized he'd said it out loud.

The old woman's chair creaked as she rocked back and forth, back and forth. Finally, when he could bear the suspense no longer, he walked through the door to the balcony. She continued rocking. James was too nervous to look at her face, so he quietly took a seat on the step that led out from the door. She didn't turn and look at him, merely taking another sip of her dark coffee.

"What's your name?" James asked quietly.

"My name?" she said. "The children used to call me Mrs. DuCrét—but that was a long, long time ago."

She coughed after the last word, and the two sat in silence for a few minutes longer. It was peaceful. They had a connection, an understanding, and there was comfort in the silence. Rionzi DuCrét and James were both people who enjoyed it and spent much of their lives quietly reflecting.

"James!"

Suddenly, the silence was broken by the sound of James's father calling his name. James slouched down a little and looked through the gaps in the balcony railing. He could see his father looking around the front of the inn for him, but he dared not answer from up here.

"You'd best be off, James," Mrs. DuCrét whispered.

He quietly tiptoed back into the old apartment. "Can I come again?" he whispered back through the door.

She nodded and gave a slight "Mm-hmm." As James reached the top of the creaky staircase, Mrs. DuCrét turned towards him. "Best not tell anyone, though."

It was the first time he had seen her face. He had half expected to see an ugly, hideous creature under that dirty shawl, but there was real beauty in her smile. He smiled back and scampered off, rather loudly, down the stairs. He was sure Mrs. DuCrét could hear his footsteps all the way down the hallway.

James's Friend

That evening, as James lay in bed, he couldn't erase the memory of the smile Rionzi DuCrét had given him. For some reason, the mysterious lady fascinated him. She was his secret.

When he fell asleep, he dreamed of adventure.

The sun shone through the window pane, bringing dusty light into the room. James awoke to his mother and father bustling around. When he rolled out of bed and got dressed, the three headed downstairs to the lobby, where a simple yet tasty breakfast was served to the guests each morning. James looked around and secretly hoped to see Mrs. DuCrét, but he was disappointed to find that the withered old lady wasn't there. He'd half expected to see her sitting in her rocking chair, staring out the window.

James's parents had made him promise not to go into the forest, at least not today. They knew it was probably too much to keep him cooped up in the inn for long, but for now they'd all agreed that he wouldn't wander off into the woods. James knew his parents were surprised at how calm he'd been when they first asked him not to leave the property. Since their move to the city, he had longed to be back in his beloved forest. Of course, they were unaware of his newfound adventures right here in the inn.

After breakfast, his parents headed out for a few hours to look at a house for sale in the village. James promised to stay out of trouble and out of the way of Saleem, who had offered to keep an eye on him while his parents were out. He picked up a book and pretended to read as his parents said goodbye, and he listened to the sound of their footsteps fading down the hallway. Then he ran to the window. Through the dusty glass, he could see them heading down the path and off into the village.

His big blue eyes shifted from calm and innocent to excited and adventurous. He tiptoed across the small room, quietly opened the door, and poked his head out into the hallway. Scanning both ways, he was pleased to see the entire corridor was clear. As he stepped cautiously out into the dim hallway, the door slammed behind him and made him jump. He froze, waiting to make sure no one had heard him. When he felt safe, he headed for the stairway.

He reached the second floor, scanned the hallway again, and, relieved to see no one around, made his way carefully along the hall until he reached the strange old door at the darkest end. He took one more glance behind him and then slipped through it. As he reached the top of the old staircase, he saw Mrs. DuCrét out on the balcony. He tiptoed quietly across the floor, not quite knowing why, as she had invited him to come again. Without a word, he stepped out on the balcony and took a seat on the step next to the rocking chair.

Mrs. DuCrét took a sip of her coffee, and he suspected she was smiling when she said, "I thought you'd be here sooner. I saw your parents leave." She didn't look at him as she spoke but continued staring out over the valley.

James simply smiled at her and said nothing.

After a minute or so, Mrs. DuCrét spoke again. "Your family is from the village, aren't they?"

"Yes."

"I recognized you. Why are you staying at the inn?"

"We just moved back from the city, but we don't have a house yet. Mom and Dad are going to look at one today."

"Did you like living in the city?"

"No!" James almost yelled. "I hated it. My classmates picked on me, and I couldn't play with my friend in the forest."

She turned suddenly and looked directly at him. "Your friend in the forest?"

He realized what he'd said. He wanted to stop there, but she seemed so interested, as if she knew what he was going to say next. "My mom told me not to talk about him. She says I'm too old for imaginary friends." He looked down, picked up a small stick at his feet, and began twiddling it in his fingers.

"You have an imaginary friend who lives in the forest?" Mrs. DuCrét said. She was growing distant, as if her hope had been dashed. She sat silently a moment and then spoke again. "Why did he not move to the city with you?"

James had to think about this for a minute. It was a good question. If his friend was only imaginary, why hadn't he moved with him? Perplexed, he said, "Well, I suppose because he lives in the forest." It was the best answer he could think of.

"Of course," she said, as if it had been a silly question to ask.

Rionzi DuCrét continued talking, but it seemed like she was speaking to no one in particular. She appeared to be sifting through the memories of time, and as she sifted, her thoughts came out aloud. James was unsure whether she even knew she was talking.

"Yes, I used to love the forest," she said, "but that day, when he asked me to go for that walk, I said no." She turned to James. Apparently, she knew he was there. "My husband, that is. He brought me back the most beautiful flowers that day. They had five deep purple petals, each as big as your hand. The centre was a big black furry ball, and the stems were the brightest green I had ever seen. He swore he had discovered a new species and we were going to be rich." She smiled, but her eyes were sad as she thought back to the memory. "You know, I'd never seen him so happy."

James was curious about the rest of the story, but he was too scared to ask. Instead, he simply said, "I've seen those flowers. They're pretty."

"Never touch them!" she said firmly.

James said nothing. He had touched them once, and they had made him very sick. How could he explain that his forest friend had saved him?

Another hour passed. They sat in silence, both inside their own imaginations, reliving their own memories. Neither could quite figure out how to tell the other about those thoughts, but James felt that if anyone would understand, it would be Mrs. DuCrét.

Return to the Forest

The next morning, James woke up before his parents and sat staring out the window. He had to return to school today, and he didn't want to. At least the kids at this school didn't pick on him as they had in the city. He didn't have any particularly close friends, but he felt safe.

His parents eventually woke up as the alarm clock began to beep. His mother walked over to the window and said "Good morning," giving James a small kiss on the cheek. James squirmed and made a face, but he secretly didn't mind when she kissed him. She put her arm around his shoulder and stared out the window. At that moment, Mrs. DuCrét hobbled down the street and off into the village.

"Honey," his mom called to his dad. "Look, she still goes for her walks."

James pretended he didn't recognize the old woman. "Who is she?"

Still watching the withered old figure walk down the street, Bella said, "She's the old lady who lives here in the inn, the one you're not supposed to disturb." She glanced at James to make sure he heard that reminder. "Her name is Rionzi DuCrét. She's lived in the village a long, long time. They say she's crazy."

In a voice that gave no hint that he knew anything about the old lady, he asked, "Does she live alone?"

His mother took a deep breath, trying to find the right words to say. "She had a husband who died a long time ago."

James stared at his mother, hoping she would say more.

"He became very ill quite suddenly," she continued, "and then he died. Mrs. DuCrét was heartbroken. One day, she went for a walk in the forest and didn't come back again for a whole year. When she did return, she told crazy stories, and the people of Nemesté decided that she had gone insane. The innkeeper at the time, Saleem's father, said he would care for her until she died. But she never dies."

"How old is she?" James asked.

"She has to be nearly one hundred and fifty," his mother answered. "They say her words and stories have magical powers. They can make you believe things that aren't real. They can make you become obsessed. Some say she must be a ghost, because no one can live that long."

David interrupted with a stern look. "That's enough fairy tales for one day. Come, James. You'll be late for school."

~

That evening at dinner, James asked his parents when he could go play in the forest. They had been back in the village for nearly a week now, and he was getting anxious.

"This weekend," Bella said, glancing over at David for reassurance. "Yes, if you like, you can take a short walk in the forest on Saturday."

When the weekend finally came, James found himself lying awake in bed as soon as the sun rose. He tried to be patient, but his skinny little body couldn't stay still. He tossed and turned for hours until his mom finally rolled over and got out of her bed. The thick duvet couldn't hold James any longer. He flung it off and practically jumped up.

"Mom, can I go now?" he said as quietly as possible, but his mother still turned to him with a look that told him to be quieter.

"Yes," she said, "if you get dressed and make sure to get some breakfast."

Later, once he had finished his breakfast, he grabbed a light jacket and set out for an adventurous day in the forest. The fog engulfed Nemesté this morning. It almost felt like he was in a dream or as if he had just opened his eyes and the world was still coming into focus. As James walked down the hill into the village, he could see his breath. It wasn't cold, but the village was right in a cloud. The fog didn't bother James at all, though.

As he got near the forest and the path leading into it, he didn't hesitate. Mist weaved in and out of the trees, and the dead leaves lining the forest floor crunched beneath his feet. He took a long deep breath to smell the damp forest, and the smell brought with it a flood of wonderful memories. He felt at home in the woods. It was a place, the only place, where he felt understood. Nobody judged the words he said or the thoughts he had. The forest just let him be. Here, surrounded by the tall trees and the thick fog, no one could tell him what was real and what wasn't.

James couldn't share this desire with anyone, but today he was hoping with all his heart to find his dear friend again. They had spent many days playing together. James feared, though, that his forest friend might be angry with him. It had been a year since he'd last said, "I'll see you tomorrow." James knew he could explain what had happened that day—if only he could find him.

That day, a year ago, he had returned home after a long walk in the forest to find the whole household in boxes. The smile on his face soon turned to tears as his parents told him he was done playing in the forest and that he was too old for imaginary friends. A moving truck had pulled up in front of the house, and, with tears streaming down his face, James had watched his mom and dad carry box after box out into the truck. He had cried through the night as he slept in a sleeping bag on the floor where his bed used to sit. The next day, they had left Nemesté.

That was what James would tell his friend if only he could find him. He spent the day in the misty forest searching high and low, under rocks and behind trees, but he saw nothing. At one point, he heard rustling in the leaves just beyond a big rock, and he ran as fast as he could, but as he reached the sound he realized it was just a small bird digging up long dew worms. James was growing tired. He sat on an old dead log and listened to the bustle of a large ant pile. Normally, James could have sat for hours, watching those ants and wondering about their lives, but his failure to find his friend made him not care about anything.

The rain began to pour down as he sat on the log. The ants quieted and made their way underground to seek shelter. It was difficult to tell whether the water that began to run down his face was the rain or his own tears. He was getting very wet, and the afternoon was getting late. He began to shiver a bit and decided it was time to head home. His hair was now completely drenched, and his clothes were soaked through. As he walked through the forest, he could feel the water seeping into his shoes. The chill in his body made him start running to try to warm up. He slipped a few times, once scraping his knee on a rock. It bled enough to run down his leg and onto his socks.

When he returned to the old inn, he was soaked. He was crying, as well, partly due to the fact that he was freezing but mostly because of disappointment. It was a good thing he was dripping wet, because no one could tell he was crying and no one would ask questions. When he found his mom, he practically collapsed in her arms. She gently put her hand on his head and suggested he take a bath to warm up. She just held her little boy as the bath filled with water. He was shivering and crying.

"Honey, why didn't you come back sooner?" she said. She stroked his wet hair out of his eyes. It didn't seem to matter to her that he was sopping wet. She just held him as her clothes began to soak through.

With a shaky voice and quivering blue lips, James said, "I didn't know I was so cold until I started to walk. I was quite far in the forest."

She smiled and hugged him tighter. As much as his parents worried over his imagination, James knew that his mother also loved his active brain. However, James could be trusted on his own. She never worried too much when he wandered off into the forest. He knew it so well that he could never get lost.

When the bath was full, his mother helped him slip out of his wet clothes and into the tub. He sat in the warm water until he wasn't shivering anymore, at least not from the cold. His body shook as he cried a little longer, wondering if he would ever find his friend again.

The First Meeting

The bells ringing from the church reminded people that it was Sunday. It was a comforting sound because it reminded James of home: this little village, with its strange mysteries, where he could be in his forest. His parents asked him if he wanted to go for a drive to the city in the valley, but he declined, claiming to be tired—which was partly true because of his failed adventure of the day before. He promised to stay out of the forest and out of trouble, so his parents left for the day.

Shortly after he finished the sandwich his mother had made for him, he walked to the dark end of the hall, through the afterthought door, and up the creaky steps. He didn't see visiting his mysterious friend on the third floor as "getting into trouble." As he reached the top of the stairs, he saw Mrs. DuCrét sitting in her chair, staring out at the world. For some strange reason, he wanted to tell her all about the day before. He wanted to tell her about the friend he used to play with. He wondered if perhaps his parents had been right. Had his friend only been imaginary? If he was, how could James be sure anyone was real at all?

James meandered out to the balcony and again took a seat on the cool cement step. He said a quick "Hi."

In her typical style, not indicating whether she was aware of his presence, Mrs. DuCrét spoke. "Did you walk in the forest yesterday, James?"

"Yes."

"Well, did you find your friend?"

Tears welled up in his eyes. He was a little embarrassed and just looked down. "No, I couldn't find him."

Another brief moment passed. James was desperately trying to hold back his tears.

Mrs. DuCrét let out a deep breath and said, "Tell me about him."

James's face lit with the biggest smile. No one had ever wanted to hear about his friend. People always told him not to talk about him, but Mrs. DuCrét wanted to hear. He wondered where he should start. "Well, he's quite short and can't run very fast," he said, "so I beat him in all our races—but maybe that's because of his funny feet. He doesn't wear shoes, you know, but probably because he wouldn't find any that fit him. He's a bit clumsy with those big feet. His skin is green. I asked him if he felt sick, but he said no. Then I asked him why his skin was green, and he didn't know. He said it was always like that. Then he laughed at my pink skin. Can you imagine?

"He had these funny pants, too, that he always wore. They were made of leaves. I tried to ask him where he got them, but he didn't even know what pants were." With each detail of his story, his voice got louder and more excited. Mrs. DuCrét didn't interrupt once, allowing him to continue.

"I tried to show him, and he laughed. He said it was funny that I could take my skin off and then put it back on and that I could change the colour whenever I wanted. He said the skin on his legs only changed colour when it got cold out, but that was only for a few months."

James finally stopped to take a breath. The relaxed, contemplative look the old lady usually had was gone. Her eyes were suddenly darting back and forth, and she shifted positions in her creaky old chair. She reached for her mug of cold coffee but dropped it, and the last dregs spilled on the balcony. She cursed and bent over to pick it up again but was very clumsy about it.

James was startled at his new friend's twitchy movements. She usually moved slowly and thoughtfully. He hoped he hadn't said anything offensive. She still said nothing, just stared straight ahead, off in another world.

James didn't know this, but the truth was that she knew exactly what he was talking about. She had seen creatures like the one he was describing, though that memory felt like another lifetime—a lifetime she'd hoped would never find her again, one she thought she had forgotten. If she was honest with herself, she had to admit that it haunted her every day and night.

The creatures had given her a drink, one she had never tasted before, which caused them to live almost three times as long as humans. Wasn't that what every human wanted, to live a long life? Rionzi wished she had never taken a sip of that sweet sap. The memories of her past haunted her, and even death couldn't come fast enough to ease the pain of her regret. Perhaps she couldn't die until she had forgiven herself. Whatever the case, she was stuck here…existing.

James spoke again, but his excitement had calmed a little. "Can you believe he made fun of my pants when his were made out of leaves? I don't think his home was actually in the forest, you know. He talked about home as if it was far away. He didn't know if he'd ever find it again. Maybe he did, though, and maybe that was why I couldn't find him. We looked for his home once. He said the floor was green and bouncy and the sky was blue and you could see forever. I thought he meant a field in the forest, and we walked all the way out there so I could show him, but he said that wasn't it. He seemed sad that day, too. I think I let him down. He told me to leave him alone for the night, but after that we were still good friends."

Rionzi interrupted him. "Who else knows about this story, James?"

"Well, I told Mom and Dad, but they told me to stop talking about him. And I told my friends at school—the other school in the city, that is. At first they thought I was inventing a new game to play at recess. They called my friend a freak and pretended we were a circus and the freak was our act. I told them to stop, but they didn't listen. I got so mad that they were making fun of my friend like that. I yelled at them, and they threw me to the ground and called me a freak, too. They said I belonged in a cage with my friend. Mom and

Dad stopped listening eventually, too. They told me he was imaginary and that I was too old for imaginary friends, so I stopped talking about him. But I think about him all the time."

Mrs. DuCrét nodded. "Hmm, yes, creatures like this, they haunt your thoughts. There's something about them that time cannot erase."

With a sigh, James said, "Yes, I suppose."

There was silence. James began to worry that he had shared too much. His mind began to wander to the first time he met his forest friend. The funny creature had actually saved his life once. Since then, James had been a bit of a social outcast. He sometimes wondered whether he would ever lead a normal life, but it seemed to him that to lead a normal life he would have to deny that his friend in the forest existed. He would have to be suspicious of everything, even his own senses, and would have to deny an experience that had shaped his life. He couldn't betray his friend like that.

The day his friend saved his life had been a normal day, just like any other. James had wandered off into the forest to throw sticks, jump logs, and climb trees. He had played pretend games of heroes and kings in distant lands. The mysterious forest had been the perfect backdrop for a mystical kingdom.

In his curiosity, James had walked into a part of the forest he had never seen before. He tiptoed along, trying very hard to be invisible, but as any creature knows, when one walks in a forest, he is rarely quiet. The fallen leaves crunched under his feet. Every few steps, he would stop and look around to make sure he was still alone, partly in his game of make believe and partly to take in his new surroundings. He made very sure to take note of the large rock along the familiar path, and as he continued deeper and deeper into the forest, he would take note of other landmarks so he wouldn't get lost.

It was in this unfamiliar part of the forest that James stumbled upon something he had never seen before. In a circle stood a random group of rocks about as tall as James. He approached the circle slowly, pretending he was approaching the castle of his enemy to embark on an attack. Between two of the rocks, the sun shone through the forest canopy, illuminating a small crack just wide enough for him to look through. Inside the enemy fortress was a small, beautiful cluster of a type of flower he had never seen before, not even in fairy tales.

The flower was a deep, rich purple. The petals were the size of his hand, and a furry black ball held them all together. The stems were the brightest green he had ever seen. Even when the sun hid behind a cloud, the stems still glowed vibrantly. He was mesmerized by the beauty he had found surrounded by rocks, and he wanted to get a better look at the flowers.

He managed to find a crack in the rocks just big enough for his scraggly little arm to fit through. He snapped off the flower and pulled it out through the crack. The scent was peculiar. It was very faint, and James had to put his nose very close to the large petals. When he took a deep breath, the smell that reached his nose was soft and pleasant. There was a sweetness and calmness to it. He closed his eyes tight to breathe in the smell and then opened them again as he exhaled.

He studied the new flower ever so carefully, not wanting to wreck a single petal. The soft black ball in the centre felt like the furry seeds of a pussy willow. The stem was thick and had snapped cleanly where James picked it. It wasn't like those flowers that he had to twist and tear at, only to get a stringy mess when he tried to pick them.

James sat quietly on a fallen log, touching, smelling, and exploring the flower. He went back to the circle of rocks. His make-believe game was over now as he explored his new discovery. He tried to pick another flower, but they were all too far away. The rocks almost seemed placed around this little bit of beauty to protect it—or to protect him. After about ten minutes, James began feeling quite ill. As he looked up, he grew dizzy. The large trees in the deep forest spun around and around. He closed his eyes for a minute to try to make the spinning stop, but when he opened them again, nothing was better.

He looked down at his hands, which were now covered in a green film. He immediately dropped the purple flower, and it almost floated down, as if gravity had no effect on it. It gently hit the ground without a sound and lay there among the dead leaves. James tried to stand up, but he fell back down right beside the purple flower. He was unsure of how long he lay there. The last thing he saw was the deadly purple flower lying beside him, almost mocking him as he began drifting in and out of sleep. He couldn't keep his eyes open any longer, and he gave in to what he assumed would be death. The flower seemed to be wilting and dying, as well.

James's memory of the incident with the purple flower was interrupted when Mrs. DuCrét spoke. As though she had read his mind, she said, "James, remember the purple flowers I talked about the other day, the ones my husband picked for me before he died?"

James nodded, still drifting out of the memory.

"The flowers...they died with him, and his hands were green. They faded as he faded."

"Yes." James understood. "I picked one once when I was in the forest. Everything went blurry and fuzzy. I thought I was going to die. That was when I met my friend. I awoke to the funniest-looking creature I had ever seen. He was giving me a drink of this sweet sap-like stuff. Suddenly, the forest came into focus, and he took my hand. His hands were fuzzy like the stem of a flower. They tickled a little. We walked over to the rocks where the purple flowers were, and he showed me something. The flower I had picked, the one that had been beside me when I blacked out, was also alive again. It was getting brighter every minute." He paused. "My hands weren't green anymore, either, but my friend's hands still were. I think they're always green."

Mrs. DuCrét smiled a little and said, "Yes, I think they are."

There was a long pause as they sat there. The two unlikely characters shared a connection and an experience that was laced with wonder and awe but also shame and regret. It was this shame and regret that brought a halt to the conversation. The fear of her haunting secrets being discovered brought out an unexpected response from Rionzi DuCrét.

"James, you will have to leave me today. I need to be alone," she said.

James was confused. "Did I say something wrong?" he said, tears welling up in his eyes.

She grabbed the collar of his shirt and brought him in so close that he could smell the rank scent of coffee on her breath. "Get out of my house for your sake, dear child! Get away from me, as far away as you can!"

James was terrified. When she let go, he stumbled backwards and fell through the open door. He looked back at her as he stood up. Her eyes were wide, and she stared right through him. He ran for the stairs and stole one last glance. She was still staring and breathing heavily.

He rushed down the stairs and pushed through the shabby door, nearly knocking it right off its hinges. As the door slammed shut, he fell beside it and wept. He was grateful there was nobody in the hall to see him. Rionzi DuCrét was the only person in the world who understood him. Why had she suddenly become so angry?

The Forbidden Word

When James returned from school, his parents were out looking at yet another house in the village. It had been almost a week since he last saw Mrs. DuCrét. Each day when James returned to the inn, he couldn't help but glance up to see if she was on the balcony. She always was, though he could only catch a glimpse of her withered figure through the slits in the railing.

Today, he stepped outside on his own balcony, which was a few floors below. He understood why she spent so much time out there. The valley provided the perfect backdrop for a person to sit and wonder about life. James had ventured off into the forest a few more times but had been unsuccessful in finding his friend. He was losing hope. He was confused.

Part of him wondered whether his parents were right. Had his forest friend only been imaginary? When he was around his parents, he buried his hopes so deep that he wondered whether he'd ever be able to find them again. In those times, he wondered whether anything was real. However, when he spent time with Mrs. DuCrét, something between them made his friend more than a make-believe companion for a lonely child.

James sat on the hard floor of the balcony, and he could hear Mrs. DuCrét's creaky old chair rocking back and forth, back and forth. Even as he sat there, close enough to hear her movements, his friend in the forest felt real. Suddenly, a thought occurred to him. Maybe Rionzi DuCrét knew his friend. He debated for a minute whether to make another attempt at talking to the mysterious lady upstairs, but he thought of a better plan. He would ask his parents. He would ask why Mrs. DuCrét—or, as he would word it, the weird lady upstairs—had been exiled to the inn. What were her crazy stories?

It seemed to take forever for his parents to return. When they finally did and the family sat down for a takeout dinner, David and Bella first talked about the house they had looked at. They were positive about it and had made an offer. That had been the excitement of their day.

Finally, the discussion wore down, and it was James's turn to talk.

"Can I ask you a question?" He continued without waiting for a response. "I caught a glimpse of that weird lady upstairs today when I was picking some berries outside. Why do they lock her up on the balcony all the time? I mean, you said she told crazy stories, but why is she stuck here?"

Bella glanced over at David. David stood up and said, "I need to go talk to Saleem about something. Try to keep the storytelling to a minimum." Then he walked out the door.

His mom turned to him. "When I was just a bit younger than you, James"—Bella wore a smile that James had never seen before—"Mrs. DuCrét's husband died and she disappeared for a while. Everyone in the village thought she was dead. When she walked back into Nemesté, it was like seeing a ghost. People asked her where she had been for so long. Her answer was always 'I've been away.' Everyone assumed she was grieving the loss of her husband.

"A group of us kids were playing in the park one day. It was sunny, and Mrs. DuCrét wandered in and sat on the bench. One boy went over to her and asked her to tell him a story. He gave her a hug and said he had missed her while she was gone."

James interrupted. "What did she say?"

"She asked him if he'd ever climbed to the top of a tree. The rest of us heard her say this and slowly crept over to hear what was next. She made up all these wonderful stories about adventures with the weirdest creatures in the treetops, where she said you could see the sky forever."

That last sentence rang in James's head. "You could see the sky forever," he whispered. That was exactly the way his forest friend had described his home. It took everything James had not to jump up and down with excitement. His mom was going on with her story, so James let her continue.

"She said that she lived with those creatures in the treetops and told us stories of how they lived and what they ate. She talked of long nights staying up, watching the sun set in the endless sky." His mother paused for a moment as she snapped back into an awareness of her surroundings. Her smile disappeared, and she remembered that she was an adult. Adults weren't supposed to believe wild stories about mythical creatures—but with that smile and the way she'd told the story, James wondered whether maybe, just possibly, his mother had believed Mrs. DuCrét. His mother continued, but the story turned from enchanting to mocking. "Our parents didn't like the stories Mrs. DuCrét was telling. Some of the kids believed in her wild creatures."

"Do you?" James asked.

"Me? When I was a child, sure. Kids believe

crazy things, you know. But think about it, James: a grieving lady leaves for a year and comes back with stories of unheard creatures? No…" There was disappointment in her voice. "No, the stories couldn't be true."

They sat in silence for a minute. James was putting together the puzzle pieces of the other day, when Mrs. DuCrét had gotten so angry with him. His mother was reliving that day long ago in the park. She remembered pretending to go on adventures with the creatures, then the horror of being picked up and dragged away by her mother. She was struggling and trying to hear more of the story over the kicking and screaming of all the other children being dragged away by their parents.

Bella looked at the door, then back at James. She leaned in really close. "Mrs. DuCrét called them Fidoris."

Did his mother sense the magical power of that word? Just then, his father walked back in the door. His mother glanced at him and put her finger over her mouth. "Shh," she whispered. The word *Fidori* was never to be mentioned in Nemesté again. James understood the importance of this and said no more.

"Are you done making up stories now?" David said with a bit of sarcasm.

James and his mom smiled at each other with the understanding that they now shared a secret. Bella nodded back at her husband.

A Magical Story

The next day, James was alone again, as his parents had gone to take another look at the house. He had to see the strange lady upstairs, and he knew what he was going to tell her. He was a little nervous as he tiptoed up the steps. He didn't want to startle her, so as he reached the top of the stairs, he knocked on the wooden railing and quietly said, "Hello? Mrs. DuCrét, are you home? It's me, James."

James could see the withered figure curled in her rocking chair. The rocking stopped. He watched her put down her stained coffee cup. She turned around, and her sunken eyes stared him straight in the face. "Why are you here? I told you to leave."

Her voice was raspy and seemed angry.

With all the strength James had, he said, "I have to ask you something."

He was already at the door that led out to the balcony before she could respond. Rionzi wouldn't admit it out loud, and she did her best not to act like it, but she was secretly happy to see the scraggly boy again. He shared her secret. They had a connection, and it had been some time since Rionzi DuCrét had felt connected to another human being. "Well, I don't see that I have much of a choice in the matter," she snapped. "Go ahead, ask your question."

James was scared, but he had to ask: "They're called Fidoris, aren't they? And you've seen them, haven't you?"

There was a pause. Mrs. DuCrét had to think about how to answer this. She knew what they were, of course, as she had lived with them for a long time, but the word Fidori brought with it such sweet memories. Rionzi knew all too well what it felt like to be the only person to know of such beautiful creatures. They were too incredible for her to leave James wondering whether they were actually real. No, she couldn't lie about them.

"Yes, James. Yes, they're called Fidoris, and yes, I've seen them before," she admitted.

James could feel himself getting angry. Why had she not said anything if she knew what he was talking about? Why had she told him to leave the last time they'd talked? James was speechless in his anger. The questions circled and circled in his mind, louder and louder.

Mrs. DuCrét spoke, but the bitterness seemed to have melted into fond memories. The very word *Fidori* seemed to carry the power to calm and bring a smile to a person's face. "Surely you're wondering why I didn't say something earlier. Well, it's difficult to explain. Not that it's an excuse, but, James, I'm not really allowed to talk about them. Oh, I've wanted to for so long. You understand the want, the need to talk about Fidoris, don't you? They're wonderful, and if only you could tell your human loved ones of the bond you can share with one of those strange creatures, perhaps humans could learn from them. But no one will believe you. Maybe the children will, but only until they're told otherwise." There was more to the story, but shame and regret kept Mrs. DuCrét from saying it.

"He's real, then?" James asked with all the hope in the world. "I mean, I didn't just make him up?"

"Him, just one?" she asked. James looked up at her. Her face was lit strangely now. She almost looked excited. "There are hundreds of them. They live on the treetops. They're a part of the trees, in a weird way."

His voice grew excited. "They live on the trees? How do you know?"

"James," she said softly, "you must remember never to tell anyone we've talked."

He nodded.

"I lived with them once." She closed her eyes and smiled. "Oh, you would love it up there. You really can see forever."

"What were they like?"

"They care for the trees playfully, the way you and I would play with a dog, and in return the trees give them the nutrients they need to live. The Fidoris have an amazing relationship with the trees. Somehow, I think humans have lost that. We take from them only what we need and rarely give back to them, but the Fidoris…they know the trees and are known by the trees. Can you imagine what it's like to be known by a tree?"

James sat forward, and his eyes grew wider with each word that poured from Rionzi's mouth.

Mrs. DuCrét continued: "When my husband passed away, I was confused. I wanted to seek the

flowers and rip each one out of the ground and trample them because they had killed him. I went to the spot where he said he had seen them. As a branch crunched under my foot, something moved in front of me. The Fidoris call her Simputus, the keeper of the death flowers. I found this out later when they told me one of their many legends. She is a long, skinny creature, and her legs are green like the Fidoris, but her top half is a deep, rich purple like the flowers. Her eyes are black as coal, and when I looked at them, I could see death.

"As I sat there, mesmerized by this thing, she suddenly jumped up with all the flowers in her arms and ran off into the forest. I began chasing her. Soon, I couldn't see her anymore, but I kept running and running. The mist grew heavy and the forest became dark, as the trees were thick. When I was worn out and I hadn't seen her in a long time, I stopped running. I was in a part of the forest I had never visited before.

"Suddenly, there was a terrible shriek, but I couldn't see anything. I stepped backwards, my eyes darting back and forth. I bumped into a tree and began climbing. I didn't know what else to do. I was so scared. I don't know how long I climbed. I had never been so high up a tree, even as a child. As I got closer to the top, I could hear noises above me. They sounded like footsteps, as though someone was running—not exactly like footsteps, though. Maybe how rabbits would sound.

"I stopped climbing to rest a minute. Nothing had followed me up the tree, so I knew this mad creature was likely far enough away that I could sit and breathe. But I couldn't help listening to the curious noises above me. It seemed like laughter and singing and dancing. At that moment, I forgot all about my hunt for the death flowers or my encounter with that creature. Fear seemed to be replaced by curiosity. I'm sure you know what that is like, James."

James smiled at Mrs. DuCrét. She had never seen his eyes so wide open as now. He was staring out, off the balcony, but his eyes were lost in imagination. He was looking out at the trees in the valley, wondering what the noise could have been. He turned and looked at her. "What was up there?" he asked.

It had been many years since the old lady told the story of her great adventure, but the magic that accompanied the creatures called Fidoris returned as she recounted the tale. Her body felt a release as she finally spoke of them again.

"I had reached the top of the tree. All that lay between me and the blue sky above was a thick canopy of leaves—very thick. It took a few minutes to wiggle my way through. When I finally did, the sun shot through the leaves with a startling blindness. I could still hear the sounds, though they were farther away now. As I pulled myself up through the gap, the most incredible scene opened up before me.

"I could see forever. I was actually able to sit on top of those thick trees. The gap closed quickly behind me, and there I was, on top of the world. It took a minute for my eyes to adjust to the brightness of the sun. The funniest thing happened next. I fell asleep on the treetops. What a beautiful place to sleep. When the wind is blowing gently through the trees, it sort of rocks you like a cradle.

"The next thing I knew, I was being wakened by some scratchy hands brushing my arms and legs. It startled me a little, but for some reason I only opened my eyes and stared at the weird creatures. I was not frightened. They weren't mean. I couldn't figure out at first what they were doing, but I later found out. You see, when Fidoris wake up in the morning, part of the trees they sleep on grows into them, and so they brush themselves off. Like I said, I didn't know this at the time, but they were trying to brush the branches off me. Now, I think I scared them a little because my skin was so smooth and there were no leaves stuck to me. The more they brushed, the more confused they seemed to be. Slowly, their brushing stopped, and I began to sit up and look around."

A car door slammed in the parking lot below the old inn. It startled both Rionzi and James.

The world of weird creatures who lived on the treetops faded away as voices from the lot reached the upper balcony.

James crept to the edge and peered through the slits in the railing. "Oh no," he whispered. "It's my mom and dad. They'll be looking for me. I have to go." The scrawny boy scampered off without waiting for a reply.

As Rionzi watched her friend go, she was saddened. How she had longed to be back amongst the dear creatures who had taught her great things. They had taught her how to relate to a tree. They had taught her that although an idea may seem crazy, it can still be true. They had taught her to respect and love and to sit and listen. She had learned to listen to the wind blow and feel the trees sway. She had stumbled upon their world in a time when she was depressed, confused, and angry about losing her dear husband. The Fidoris knew of her struggles, as they too had suffered loss at the hands of Simputus and her purple flowers. She hadn't said the word *Fidori* out loud in nearly forty years. It brought with it such wonder and beauty. The sweet memories that had come flooding back as she told James her story were so powerful that in that moment, she had forgotten the bitter ending that controlled most of her life. To have such joy in simple, sweet memories was something Rionzi hadn't felt in a long time. How could such a small, curious boy bring about such happiness? Perhaps this was a result of their rare shared experience. She tried to close her eyes and hold on to the memories just a bit longer, but as she breathed in the familiar smells of the old inn, the images disappeared and the bitterness returned.

Her breathing grew heavy, and she squinted at the bright sun. Normally, the view over the valley brought some form of peace to her restless heart, but today it seemed to have the opposite effect, because it had brought her out of her sweet memories.

~

James bumped into his parents on the stairwell from the second floor.

"James!" his father said with excitement. "Come, son, we've got some great news for you."

When they reached the small room that had been home for the past few weeks, David picked James up and plopped him down on the big double bed. He then spun around, laughing, and looked James straight in the eye.

"James, my boy, we're going home!" He glanced over at Bella, and they smiled at each other. "We bought a house, yes we did!"

James sat, staring in silence, letting the news soak in.

"What do you think?" David said, too excited to notice James pondering. "We'll get out of this dingy, crowded hotel room and have a yard to run around in instead of a dusty inn. How does that sound?"

Suddenly, James realized he had been asked a question. He answered, "Yes, that sounds good." He tried to put on a convincing smile, but he was torn. The thought of having a large yard to run around in was appealing, but he remembered his friend upstairs. Though she was full of mystery, she understood his dearest secrets. Also, she hadn't finished her story of the Fidoris. Would he see her again?

"One week, James! One week until we move out of this dump," David said. He didn't tell James this at first, but the house they had bought was on the edge of town, with its backyard leading right into the old forest.

That night, unknown to each other, both Rionzi DuCrét and James were haunted by dreams of Simputus and all her evil. This wasn't the first time she had visited the village. This strange creature was very old and had haunted the streets of Nemesté since its existence. The humans had destroyed everything she and others like her had lived for. Simputus was the only purple flower keeper left now, and her anger drove her to seek revenge in any way she could.

In Rionzi's dream, she was on the treetops, searching for the Fidoris. She couldn't find them, though, and an uneasy feeling came upon her.

She looked around, and out of nowhere, the gangly green hand of Simputus reached through a beamer—the word Fidoris used for the holes in the canopy floor, which they tried to avoid. The beamer had just appeared, and the hand began dragging Rionzi down into the darkest depths of the forest. She tried with all her might to free her leg from Simputus's grasp, but the hand kept pulling and pulling.

When they stopped, Rionzi was too stunned to move. She finally opened her eyes to find that she was surrounded by the purple flowers. They swayed in the wind, and the black middles stared at her. She couldn't see Simputus, but she could feel her all around. The flowers began growing closer and closer to her curled-up body. She yelled and screamed, but they kept growing. Just as the flowers were about to swallow her, Rionzi awoke from her sleep. Her sheets were drenched in sweat, and the room slowly came into focus.

This wasn't the first time Rionzi had had dreams where the black eyes of Simputus stalked her. The feeling of fear she had encountered so long ago in the darkest part of the forest was unique to any other fear. To meet a creature that could only embody evil, with no hope of redemption, was a terrifying feeling. The powers of grace, love, hope, and truth held nothing over Simputus. When her black eyes met Rionzi's, the old woman had been tempted to believe the same about herself. This was a frightening thought.

James had a similar dream that night. He had never met Simputus, so he didn't understand it completely, but he had once been touched by her evil flowers, and it was those vibrant purple flowers with their mesmerizing black centres that imposed on his dreams. He wanted to pick a bouquet for Mrs. DuCrét, but the only flowers he could find were the purple ones.

He had gone back to their new house, and there was a huge bouquet on the table. When he saw the flowers, James screamed, but his mother only looked at him, smiling. The black balls reflected in her eyes and made them look black, just the way

Mrs. DuCrét had described Simputus. James ran and ran, but everywhere he went the flowers were there: on the path, in the field, and behind each rock. He tripped and fell, and when he stood up, he realized he had fallen right on top of a huge circle of them.

The strange feeling he remembered from when he first picked the flower, when the world seemed to fade into darkness, began overpowering him. Just before he faded, he woke up, screaming. His mom came quickly to his bedside. He was sitting straight up and staring at her with fear. She calmly put her arms around him. He realized it had been a terrible nightmare and cried into his mother's shoulder.

"It was just a bad dream, honey," she said to him. "There, there, just a bad dream."

They sat this way for a while until James's breathing grew slower and calmer. Once he had settled down, his mother went back to her own bed. He assured her he would be fine, but he couldn't sleep the rest of the night.

The Edge of the Hedge

uring the next week, David and Bella were out every day, sorting out the new house. When James woke up on Saturday morning, he was alone. His parents had left him some breakfast and lunch and said they would be back to take him out to dinner. There was little hesitation as to where James would spend his day. He scurried up the stairwell to the third floor.

"Oh, sorry, sir," James said as he rounded the corner, nearly knocking over the innkeeper.

"Whoa! Good morning, James. I hear you'll be leaving us soon," Saleem said.

James stopped. He had been taught to listen to adults when they were speaking to him. "Um, yes, sir."

The innkeeper could tell James was in the middle of an important game. "Well, off you go, then."

"Thank you. Goodbye, sir." James was relieved at the shortness of the conversation, and he scurried off down the corridor. He took a quick look over his shoulder to be sure that Saleem had left the hallway. Then he quietly opened the old door at the end of the hall and made his way up the creaky staircase.

Walking up those stairs was something James had to do slowly. It was almost as if the walk built his suspense. At the top, he would find the unlikely friend who'd captured his imagination. He could spend hours listening to her stories. They had only made it as far as the tops of the trees the last time they met, when James had suddenly been forced to leave. He had waited days to see Mrs. DuCrét again, because with each new story she told him, more memories of his friend were flooding back.

The walk up the stairs was the beginning of his adventure. As he reached the top, he peered out to the old veranda and made his way towards the withered old figure that rocked back and forth.

"James," she said with a smile, "I was wondering when you'd be coming back."

"Mrs. DuCrét, Mom and Dad bought a house on the other side of the village. I may not be able to visit much more." James had to hold back tears.

"I feared this time would come. When do you leave?" she asked.

"Three days." He paused a moment. "The house is at the edge of the forest."

Rionzi appeared to ignore this comment, but in truth, she would never forget it. She knew the house. "Well, James, do you want to hear more about the Fidoris?"

James took his usual seat on the step out to the balcony. Across the valley, a storm seemed to be blowing in. The sun still peeked through, but the sky was darkening by the minute. The clouds were building, and he could hear echoes of thunder in the distance. As they watched the scene, James slowly began to imagine being on the treetops.

"What odd-looking creatures they were," Rionzi began. "I'd never even heard of them in all the old fairy tales. Their bodies were similar to ours, but their skin was green, with little twigs and leaves growing off it. You remember your friend's legs? That was where the leaves were thickest. They looked like pants. On top of their heads, the leaves were thick or not so thick depending on age. You know how hair grows on our heads? It's similar with them, only they have leaves. James, you remember when you told me your friend had those big clumsy feet?"

"Yeah!" James excitedly jumped in. "They looked like big mushrooms, only upside down."

"Yes," Rionzi continued with a smile, "those big mushroom feet. You know, up on the trees, it's our feet that look silly and clumsy. The Fidoris can bounce along the trees very quickly with those huge feet, and it looks so fun. I couldn't keep up. My little feet kept falling between the branches. They thought my feet were small and clumsy. They thought, how silly to have such small feet. We eventually made some big feet for me out of some branches. They didn't bounce like the big mushroom feet of the Fidoris, but I could at least run along without falling through the foliage. Do you remember when I told you they were brushing my arms when I woke up?"

James nodded.

"Each morning, when the Fidoris wake up, they spend about half an hour brushing the branches off themselves. You see, when they sleep, they sort of burrow into the canopy, and the branches grow up around them to keep them warm. They can't sleep for more than twelve hours, though, or they might grow right into the trees. They had watched me sleep for more than twelve hours, so they were brushing me off, and that was when I woke up. I could hardly remember how I got there, I was so exhausted.

"I found out about Simputus shortly after waking up. When the Fidoris noticed the branches weren't attached to me, they were a bit nervous. Besides the birds that fly overhead and the Fidoris themselves, they only know of one other creature. Most of what they know about her is from a legend. In fact, the oldest Fidori, their leader, who's called Motumbu, is the only Fidori among them now to have ever seen Simputus. He doesn't like to speak of her."

James's eyes were bulging out of his head. He looked at Rionzi with intensity and asked, "What's the legend?"

"It goes like this: two Fidoris, Fondor and Sion, were off exploring the treetops. There are spaces in the trees called beamers, and the forest below is so dark that it swallows up the light. The Fidoris are told not to get too close to them because they could fall into the unknown blackness. One day, Fondor and Sion came across a beamer and decided to look into it. This was where they met Simputus. At the exact same time they were looking down the hole, she was looking up at them.

"At first, they thought she was a Fidori who had fallen in, and they pulled her up to the top. They soon realized she wasn't. She was skinnier than most Fidoris, and she struggled to walk along the tops of the trees because her feet weren't bouncy mushrooms. Hers were more like wavy flower petals. She seemed friendly despite her black eyes, and she could sense their overpowering curiosity, so she told them something no Fidori had ever

imagined doing. 'You can bounce off the edge to the hedge,' she said. Bounce off the edge to the hedge! What a strange concept. Fidoris always stayed away from the edge of the forest because they couldn't see what was beyond it, but Simputus said it wasn't that far down, and they could bounce off and then back up.

"That night, when Fondor and Sion returned home, they couldn't get that simple rhyme out of their heads. The edge to the hedge…it seemed so simple and innocent, only something to spark curiosity. Unbeknownst to them, Simputus's intentions were far from good and pure. She knew it was a far drop, and a Fidori would die if he or she jumped off. From time to time, Simputus had seen the adventurous Fondor and Sion running away from their group. They would invent endless make-believe games while exploring, bouncing higher and higher and pretending there were beamers all over, with monsters waiting to drag them down. But in all their games, never once had they imagined what lay beyond the edge of the hedge. For a human, James, it would be like believing you could breathe under water.

"The next day, Fondor and Sion went back to the beamer where they had seen Simputus. Nobody knows exactly what happened. Some say they found the edge of the hedge and fell off. Others say Simputus dragged them down the beamer into her dark world. But they were never seen again. Since Fondor and Sion's mysterious disappearance, Simputus has been seen from time to time, but the accounts are vague—like turning around only to see a dark shadow disappear, or the sense of being watched as one passes a beamer. The name Simputus has sometimes been used to define the concept of evil.

"The Fidoris searched all over the treetops for Fondor and Sion. At each beamer, they would cautiously look into its blackness, but there was no sign of them. One day, Motumbu wandered off on his own to search when he saw a strange creature hobbling along over the treetops. Curious, he yelled at the creature to stop. Startled, the withered old thing looked up. This was when Motumbu saw her black eyes. She began hobbling faster away from him, heading for a beamer. Before Motumbu could reach her, she slipped down into the darkness. He looked down and watched her deep purple hair disappear. That is why he cringes at the sound of her name. You can almost see her black eyes reflecting from his, but perhaps this is because I have seen those black eyes, too."

"Almost like the black balls in the centre of the purple flowers," James blurted out.

Rionzi DuCrét had never thought of this, but she suddenly made the connection. When she glanced into Simputus's black eyes, she'd had one of those déjà vu moments but hadn't been able to figure out why. It suddenly clicked now. Looking at Simputus's eyes was like looking at the flowers her husband had brought back for her that devastating day so long ago.

She finally answered James. "Yes, very much so." There was another small pause. "Well, that is the legend of Simputus. No Fidori is quite sure who she is, what she is, or where she is from. The idea of evil didn't really exist for those beautiful creatures before Simputus, but they know it now. They know the pain that stems from misunderstanding and injustice."

"What is Motumbu like? Is he a good king?" James wondered.

"Indeed, he is. He cares very much for the wellbeing of his subjects. His wife, Aliumbra, is the most beautiful Fidori of them all. Her large mushroom feet are the brightest, and they almost shine. She has great big eyes that stare through you, almost as if reading your heart. Many Fidoris seek her wisdom. The leaves on her head always seem to fall perfectly in place. She and King Motumbu tell elaborate stories together, each reciting different parts. Even the trees they step on seem to know and respect them."

"What do the Fidoris do all day?"

"They take care of the trees, removing the dead branches and leaves, and they spend hours collecting sap to make a sweet drink that's said to have power even greater than that of Simputus. Some of the dead branches they eat, and others they save for the evening. Do you like campfires, James?"

"Oh, yes, I do," he replied.

"Well, as you can imagine, it would be quite dangerous to have a campfire on the top of a tree. But their evening ritual reminds me of a campfire. They dip their collected dead branches in the sap. Then they stick them in the ground—or, rather, the treetop floor. The moon shines on them, making them glow in the dark. The Fidoris' dancing is something you can't imagine. Because of their mushroom feet and bouncy treetops, they can jump higher and higher. Once they get tired of dancing, they all huddle together around the glowing sticks and tell great stories. We would all eventually lie down, tangled with one another, burrowing into the trees, and drift off to sleep. It's difficult to feel lonely with the Fidoris. And, like I said, the trees sway and rock you at night."

"That sounds wonderful," James said.

"It's so different from the cruel world of humans. Here, we all sleep in our own houses and beds, far, far away from one another and detached from anybody else. It's no wonder we feel lonely. Fidoris live for a long time, you know, nearly three hundred years. I think it's the sap they drink. It has a weird magic to it, but it's not meant for us humans."

"Why not? What would happen if we were able to live that long?" James asked.

"I guess our lifestyles would have to change. I don't mean just environmentally, although that would need to be part of the change, as well. I think, more importantly, the way we relate to one another. Forgiveness, grace, love, and justice—we would have to do all these things better. There couldn't be ulterior motives. You see, with time, such motives are always exposed. You can't hide behind fake love forever. The beauty of the Fidoris doesn't allow it. Can you imagine a world where we purely forgave, purely allowed for grace, purely loved, and were purely just?"

James was thinking about what Mrs. DuCrét was saying, trying to understand.

"The Fidoris, James"—she continued without waiting for his answer—"they know how to love. They should be allowed to live for that long. I've lived a long life, and I fear I have more to live, but it has been a life of scars and loneliness."

James could understand that. He had lived a similar life, although much shorter, and perhaps his scars weren't quite as deep. He seemed to still have hope in people. Perhaps this was the beautiful innocence of childhood.

Rionzi DuCrét continued: "Humans can be nasty to one another, but, James, we can also be nasty to ourselves. This makes life all the lonelier. Anyway, I probably shouldn't say these things. I'm a bitter old lady, bitter at the world, bitter at the way I've been treated, and bitter at the terrible sins I've committed." A single tear rolled down her wrinkly cheek.

James caught sight of it glistening as it dripped off and splashed into a star shape on the wood of the balcony. He might not have grasped the extent of what Mrs. DuCrét was trying to say—in fact, she was making little sense to him at all—but he recognized tears, and they usually came when something hurt.

The story had come to a sudden end with her tears. Rionzi had drifted off into loneliness, and James didn't know what to say. Every few minutes, another tear would splash to the ground with the faintest sound. James watched the interesting shapes the tears made on the wood.

The silence was broken with Mrs. DuCrét's voice, softer than usual. "I'm out of stories today, James," she said.

"But my friend is real?" he asked with all the hope in the world.

"Yes, more real than most things people say. Keep looking for him, James." She put her rough, wrinkly fingers under his chin and lifted his head to look him in the eye. The touch startled him a little. "You don't have much of a choice. It's magic or beauty or perhaps both. You'll always be looking for him, but promise me this: when you move and you find your friend, will you remember me?"

He looked at her as if she was crazy. "How could I forget you?" he said a little too loudly.

She put her finger over his mouth. "Shh. Then off you go. I know we shall see each other soon."

Rionzi Grows Suspicious

The house James and his family moved into was an old log home right beside the forest. James's new room looked out over the large yard and into the trees, and he often found himself staring out the window, hoping to see his funny-looking friend wobbling along the path. Any noise he heard made him run to the window, but it was usually just a bird or a squirrel fussing around in the leaves.

One day, as the clouds rolled in and blanketed the village, James heard a short tap on his window. He glanced out and saw nothing, but as soon as he turned his attention back to his toys, he heard it again. This time, he stood and walked over to the window. The fog was so thick that he barely noticed the withered figure at the back of the yard. It took him a second to realize who it was, as he had never seen her standing before.

She was wearing a long charcoal coat, black rubber boots, and a deep purple scarf to cover her ragged grey hair. The fog wisped around her almost as if she were a ghost. She looked up at the window, and James recognized her right away. He had only seen her eyes a few times, but he could never forget the intensity and understanding they held.

James wanted to go on her walk with her. Oh, how he missed his unlikely friend. He longed to hear the word *Fidori* again. She was still staring at him and seemed to be begging him to come, so he wasted no time in scurrying down the stairs and grabbing his coat.

"Mom!" he yelled. "I'm going to play outside."

"Okay, honey," she yelled back, distracted by something else.

The screen door slammed as he practically jumped down the three steps from the deck to the ground. He looked up to where Mrs. DuCrét had been standing, but she was no longer there. He ran towards the forest, the fog breaking in front of him.

"James," Rionzi's familiar voice called from behind a tree. "Over here."

He was a little out of breath, but he was relieved to see the old lady.

"I'm going on a walk," she said. "Would you like to come?"

"Yes!" His eyes were filled with excitement.

They wandered off into the deep forest with the fog closing in around them. No words were needed. Both had the same hope, though for different reasons, as they meandered through the forest. They hoped to find a Fidori.

"I've missed you," James said shyly.

Rionzi hadn't been told that in a very long time. James couldn't see it, but she smiled, perhaps wider than she had in forty years.

James was surprised at how fast Mrs. DuCrét could walk for her age. They strolled deep into the forest, further and further into the fog. Alone, James had only gone this far a few times: the time when his friend had saved his life and the time he'd gone back to look for him. A large rock that looked somewhat like a house marked an invisible line in the forest. Beyond it, there was an eerie feeling that would crawl up James's spine. It felt like he had entered a space he wasn't allowed to be in. The mist made it even more creepy.

"Beyond this rock, James, is the deepest, darkest part of the forest," Rionzi said. "It is where I met evil, the keeper of the purple flowers, Simputus. Her presence guards it."

They had both stopped walking and were staring off into the blackness, afraid to take one more step.

"This is where I found the purple flowers and met my friend," James whispered, "but I've only ever gone back there once more, when I came back to look for him."

"You know, James, I'm confused," Rionzi suddenly confessed. "You speak of the same creatures I do, yet you've never been to the tops of the trees, and they've never ventured closer to the ground than the edge of a beamer." Her voice suddenly grew suspicious. "How is it that you came to see one?"

"He found me!" James almost yelled. He'd had this argument before with his parents, who'd said he was lying. Until she asked this question, James had felt Mrs. DuCrét trusted him completely.

But Rionzi DuCrét was suddenly suspicious that the village people were playing a cruel trick on her: send a cute boy to talk to her about her beloved creatures, then finally be rid of her for talking about them again. At least this was how she deceived herself to avoid the inevitable question James might bring up—a question that would force Rionzi to face her past.

"James, with your sweet little face and sad story about the kids at school picking on you, you had me fooled. I actually began to trust you with all this. You surprised me with what you knew about the Fidoris, and I thought for sure you must have seen them. But you couldn't have because they don't live on the forest floor. You're just like everyone else in this village. You are trying to get rid of me too."

"I am not! I have seen him! Why don't you believe me?" James shouted. His face was growing red with anger as he tried to hold back tears.

She stood up as straight as her old body would allow and looked down at James, pointing at him with her bony finger. Her finger shook, and although it could have been because of her age, being that she was one hundred and fifty, it was likely because of conflicting emotions. Suddenly, she became unsure of her accusation towards the shaking scrawny boy who had tears streaking down his face. Either he was telling the truth and, by some unlikely circumstance, he had seen a Fidori, or he was a very good liar.

Rionzi DuCrét could never forget the pain that had ripped through her when the people in the village stopped her from telling her stories to the children. Lies of betrayal that are passed down through generations seem to grow over time, but could this child, who was driven by emotion, really be capable of such deceit? All the sense in the world screamed no, but Rionzi was too afraid to believe it.

Suddenly, boiling over with pain and anger, James yelled as loud as he could, "Zintar is real! He saved my life! He's real!"

The little boy began to run away back towards Nemesté, and Rionzi could hear him crying as he did so. She could not stop him, because she was in shock. She had never mentioned the name Zintar to a single soul.

"How can this be?" she murmured. "The only way James could know the name Zintar is if he's met him…but this doesn't make any sense. Zintar is dead. I told him he could climb down the beamers, and he fell to his death. I killed him."

Acknowledgements

First, I would like to thank my good friend Blake Allen. Together, we created the creatures called Fidoris while sitting on the "edge of the hedge" to prune the 15 foot high hedges in our village. I spent many evenings on the balcony of a Swiss chalet, reading each new installment of the story to him by candlelight. I could not have written this story without his imaginative contribution to the creation of the characters. Thank you to Destinée Media for publishing my first book. I am grateful to Ralph and Valerie for their willingness to invest in me as an author. A big thanks to Amanda Kramer Kaczynski for her amazing illustrations! She brought this story to life with her creativity/imagination. Thank you to Devon Brown for the cover design and to Julie Lundy for putting the interior together. There were many people who helped with editing this book. The first read through was done by my Aunt Lin who bravely took the first look. Val McCall from Destinée Media passed along suggestions that helped me as I considered the character development and general flow of the story. I would also like to thank Barb Falk for spending many hours reading through and editing a slightly better version of the story. Jeannie Blair was always there to answer questions, give me an honest opinion, and edit the small odds and ends that needed a sharper eye than mine. Thanks to Talia Leduc for doing the final cover-to-cover edit.

I would also like to thank Miss Blair's Grade 5 class, who became my first young audience to hear the book. They had great questions for me about being a writer and some thoughtful suggestions to help make the story more understandable. Finally, I would like to thank my family. Thank you for reading the story, expressing interest in my writing projects and for encouraging me along the way.

About the Author

Jasmine Fogwell grew up in the small town of Norland, Ontario. She spent many years living in a village in the mountains in Switzerland that inspired *The Fidori Trilogy*. She enjoys skiing, hiking, reading and writing.

About the Illustrator

Amanda Kramer Kaczynski is originally from Eugene, Oregon. She enjoys reading, travel, and meeting new people, as well as making art of many different kinds. She has also lived in the mountains of Switzerland, where she met her husband, Kyle. They live in Madison, Wisconsin

A SNEAK PEAK OF

BOOK 2:
THE PURPLE
FLOWER

~

Rionzi Breaks the Rules

aleem sat in the lobby of the inn, staring out towards the forest. He could only see darkness beyond the quaint streetlights. His thoughts wandered. Inside, he was torn. Rionzi DuCrét had a very strict curfew for her walk. In the forty years he and his father had been responsible for her, she had never even thought of disobeying the rules that governed her limited walk in the forest once every two weeks. The penalty for breaking this condition was banishment. Some of the more vocal village people threatened banishment even to Saleem, and he feared his neighbours' responses if anyone found out she had disappeared—but, on the other hand, he could be free of her if she simply didn't come back.

For a few brief minutes, this new sense of freedom felt good, but a part of him would deeply miss the old lady. Although they rarely spoke, her presence in the inn, which was a place of constant transition, was a comfort for him. He was fascinated by her, in a way—by her extreme old age, for one thing. Despite her bitter facade, she seemed to hold on to hope. He wasn't sure what she hoped for, but he could feel it when, on rare occasions, he would run into her.

Clouds had covered the sky, and lightning flashed in the distance. A storm was blowing in, bringing rain across the valley. Finally, Saleem spotted a shadow in the dim streetlight that could be none other than Rionzi DuCrét. The way she wobbled along with her cloak covering her face, hunched over but still full of strength, was very distinct.

Water dripped off her coat as she reached the front door. She stomped the mud off her worn old boots. There were holes all over them, and inside her socks were brown and wet. The door creaked as she pushed through. The sound of rain splashing on the pavement grew as she entered. She closed the door quietly behind her, wiped her feet again, and hobbled towards the stairs. Each step creaked as she made her way up. Saleem sat beside the window and watched as she passed. If she saw him there, she didn't acknowledge it. He couldn't figure out why, but she looked more worn than usual. It could have been that she'd been out hours longer, but Saleem sensed it was more. Something was bothering her. He made his way to bed and fell asleep to wandering thoughts of what could be bothering the unique woman.

Alone in her quiet room on the third floor of the old inn, Rionzi DuCrét cried and then drifted off into a restless sleep.

At the other end of town, James was crying, as well. After Mrs. DuCrét accused him of lying about Zintar, James had run all the way back to his house and sat at the edge of the forest to finish crying before going inside. His mother noticed he was upset but didn't bother him too much about it, and James cried himself to sleep that night.

The week went by, and James was consumed with hatred for Rionzi DuCrét. It was a hatred brought on by confusion over their friendship. The shared experience of the Fidoris had created such a deep bond that he couldn't help but hate her. He was hurt, crushed, and the only way he could keep from crying all day was to be angry. Anger is a bit easier to handle than the pain of betrayal. At school, James was acting out, and at home he barely spoke. He took walks in the forest, kicking rocks, breaking sticks, and destroying the wildflowers. A few times, the pain was so fierce that anger couldn't even cover it, and he would lie down beside a tree, weeping.

During this same week, Rionzi DuCrét sat on her creaky balcony at the old inn, worried. She knew she had crushed her dearest friend. James was the only person in the world who understood her. She needed to talk to him. She needed to apologize for lashing out. She needed to beg him for forgiveness.

Rionzi had believed Zintar to be dead. After all these years, was it really possible that he was alive? She needed to see James again, but how? Would he speak to her? She tried to imagine herself in James's shoes. Would she talk to herself? Probably not, but she had to try. She could wait for him in the forest. He would come eventually, unless he was so crushed that even the forest brought no comfort. Her next walk wasn't until the following week, but she needed to see him before then. Perhaps she could sneak out in the darkness before dawn and return late into the night. It was possible nobody would notice. The thought of disobeying her contract was terrifying. She had never even considered it before, but it needed to be done. The truth of the Fidoris was too precious to be lost any longer. This was the best plan she could think of. Tomorrow was Saturday, and James would surely be out in the forest.

Rionzi DuCrét woke up at four a.m. It was still dark out. As she walked down the stairs, she was sure every guest would hear what, to her, sounded like elephants tramping through the building. But as she stepped out into the parking lot, she glanced back and noticed that no lights had come on. The thick dew of the morning sent a chill through the old lady. Rionzi put her scarf over her head and walked down through the sleeping Nemesté. Her footsteps echoed off the old cement houses. The fog wisped through the dim light given off by the streetlamps. Not a soul seemed to be awake at this hour, for which Rionzi was grateful. She reached the edge of the village and stood in the shadows, staring at James's house. Would he come out today?

**To find out what happens to
James and Rionzi, be sure to read
The Purple Flower,
Book 2 of The Fidori Trilogy!**

CPSIA information can be obtained
at www.ICGtesting.com
Printed in the USA
LVOW12s0824310816

502455LV00001B/20/P